...ENCE DETECTIVES

...e Crooked Carnival

(and Other Super-Scientific Cases)

MICHELE TORREY

ILLUSTRATED BY
BARBARA JOHANSEN
NEWMAN

STERLING

New York / London
www.sterlingpublishing.com/kids

D0089421

To Nav, Mehra, Andrea, and Katie,
whose brilliance and creativity
are quite astonishing.
M. T.

For my guys: Phil, Dave, Mike, and Ben.
B. J. N.

STERLING and the distinctive Sterling logo are registered
trademarks of Sterling Publishing Co., Inc.

Library of Congress Cataloging-in-Publication Data Available

Lot #:
2 4 6 8 10 9 7 5 3
01/11

Published by Sterling Publishing Co., Inc.
387 Park Avenue South, New York, NY 10016
Text © 2010 by Michele Torrey
Illustrations © 2010 by Barbara Johansen Newman
Distributed in Canada by Sterling Publishing
C/o Canadian Manda Group, 165 Dufferin Street
Toronto, Ontario, Canada M6K 3H6
Distributed in the United Kingdom by GMC Distribution Services
Castle Place, 166 High Street, Lewes, East Sussex, England BN7 1XU
Distributed in Australia by Capricorn Link (Australia) Pty. Ltd.
P.O. Box 704, Windsor, NSW 2756, Australia

Printed in Canada

Sterling ISBN 978-1-4027-4965-0

For information about custom editions, special sales, premium and
corporate purchases, please contact Sterling Special Sales Department
at 800-805-5489 or specialsales@sterlingpublishing.com.

CONTENTS

One • Gloom and Doom
1

Two • Ghosts and Ghouls
6

Three • The Gory Details
13

Four • Alien Invasion
20

Five • A Pleasant Outing?
27

Six • Step Right Up!
33

Seven • The Winner!
40

Eight • Fun-O-Wama
46

Nine • Danger in the Air
53

Ten • Bridge Gone Bananas
58

Activities and Experiments for Super-Scientists
67

CHAPTER ONE

Gloom and Doom

Dawn had barely cracked in the small town of Mossy Lake. A few squirrels sleepily rubbed their eyes. Mostly, though, the town was still asleep on this early, lazy Saturday morning.

But in one particular house, up the stairs and in the attic, all was astir. Beakers boiled. Solutions swirled. And electrical currents flowed.

In the center of it all stood Drake Doyle. Now one might think he was mad, in the mad scientist sort of way. His cinnamon-colored hair stood straight up, as if he'd slept upside down. He wore a lab coat. He stared through the apparatus in front of him as if he'd unlocked the secret to brain transference. Or Martian communication.

But Drake was no mad scientist. No indeed.

1

He flipped the switch. He said, "Aha!" and scribbled in his lab notebook.

Just then, the phone rang. Who would be calling at such an hour? Perhaps it was because his business cards said to call anytime:

Doyle and Fossey:
Science Detectives
call us. anytime. 555-7822

Drake and his partner, Nell Fossey, were the best amateur science-detective geniuses in the fifth grade (besides being best friends). They had a long list of satisfied customers and cases solved.

And that's why, on this early, lazy Saturday morning Drake picked up the phone: "Doyle and Fossey."

"Uh—uh, hello? Is this Detective Doyle?"

Drake's heart sank. It was Edgar Glum, the gloomiest kid in school. Edgar never told jokes. Edgar always wore black. If someone passed out cupcakes on their birthday, he'd say, "I only got one."

But, sinking heart or not, Drake was a professional, and professionals never lose heart entirely. "Ah, yes, Mr. Glum. What can I do for you?"

"Woe is me. I have a problem. I'm hearing ghosts and ghouls at night."

By this time, Drake and Nell were considered ghost experts. Even so, Drake's heart still skipped a beat. "Ghosts and ghouls, you say?"

"Their moaning and howling and clanking have kept me awake for a month. Oh, woe," Edgar sighed drearily. "I suppose you won't take the case. I'll have to call James Frisco."

Frisco! While Drake only *appeared* to be a mad scientist, James Frisco was the real deal. Frisco splashed and spilled chemicals, while Drake carefully poured them. Frisco made paper airplanes out of instructions, while Drake carefully read them. Frisco's favorite scientist was Dr. Frankenstein, while Drake's was Dr. Einstein. (In fact, Frisco's mother was still having nightmares following Frisco's latest attempt to reanimate dead cockroaches.) So you see, Frisco was a very bad, very mad scientist indeed:

FRISCO
~~bad~~ mad scientist
(Better than Doyle and Fossey)
Call me. Day or night. 555-6190

Drake could never let Frisco take the case! "Never fear, Mr. Glum. No ghost or ghoul is too frightful for Doyle and Fossey!"

Drake hung up and called Nell. "Edgar Glum's got ghosts and ghouls. We must investigate."

"You do know, Detective Doyle, that Edgar lives in the dreariest, spookiest house in town?"

"Check."

Click.

The Glum mansion was indeed the dreariest, spookiest house in town. Porches sagged. Gnarled trees loomed overhead.

Now Drake might have lost heart entirely had it not been for Nell, who, as usual, was the first to arrive, ready for business. Her coffee-colored hair was pulled back into a ponytail, and she had a pencil behind her ear. "Ready, Detective Doyle?"

"Ready."

Together they stepped onto the sagging front porch and rang the doorbell.

After a few tense moments in which Drake thought he felt something tickling the back of his neck, the door opened.

It was Edgar, looking as if he'd just eaten a lump of cold oatmeal. "You rang?"

CHAPTER TWO
Ghosts
and Ghouls

Inside, Edgar's home was dark and creepy. Yellowed wallpaper peeled from the walls. A rickety staircase led upward into the shadows. A chilly draft crept through the hall, smelling like mummies and wet socks.

If truth be told, Drake wished with all his heart that he could turn right around and pedal like mad toward home. However, being the professional that he was, he merely said (and a bit too loudly), "Nice place."

"I suppose," sighed Edgar.

Just then, something brushed against Drake from behind. He gave a little yelp, much relieved when he saw it was only a dog.

"That's Poe," said Edgar.

Poe's license tags jangled as Drake patted him. "Good doggie."

Nell whipped out her notebook and pencil and began to take notes. "Dogs can often sense ghosts and ghouls. Has Poe noticed anything unusual?"

Edgar shook his head. "He's almost blind, and mostly deaf. Plus, he stopped sleeping with me in my room on the same night the ghosts and ghouls started howling. Now he sleeps next to our new furnace in the basement. I'm all alone."

Ignoring the chill in the air, Drake whipped out his notebook and pencil as well. "The haunting started one month ago, you say?"

Edgar nodded.

"Has anything else happened in the past month?" asked Nell. "Anything unusual?"

"Well, not unless you count the chandelier crashing to the floor, and my pet tarantula dying. Now it's just my grandmother, Poe, and me."

Drake jotted furiously: *Poe won't sleep in Edgar's room anymore, chandelier crashed, tarantula died, house could use a little cheering, new wallpaper maybe. . . .*

Edgar licked his lips nervously. "Do you . . . do you think it's a ghost? A *real* ghost?"

"Impossible to tell at this point," said Drake.

"Let's take a look around," said Nell.

And so they did. They shone their flashlights in this corner and that one. They stole up and down the rickety stairs. They opened the creakity door to the attic and peered under sagging beds and in cluttered closets. They inspected the broken chandelier. They said "hello" and "nice day, isn't it?" to Edgar's grandmother, who sat knitting in the living room, listening to the radio. And finally, they headed down the stairs and into the basement, where Poe was already taking a nap.

"Nothing supernatural so far," said Drake, tripping on a step.

"Roger that," replied Nell, catching Drake by his lab coat. "Even the chandelier appears to have fallen because the cord was old and frayed."

"Well," said Drake, "at least it's warm and toasty down here."

Edgar nodded gloomily. "Like I said, we got a new furnace. Now I have to add wood to it twice a day. It's such a chore."

"Better than being cold," Nell said, as she shone her flashlight about, illuminating cobwebs, old open pipes, dusty boxes, and rusty bicycles.

"I suppose," sighed Edgar.

Then, just as Drake was warming his hands near the furnace, a strange thing happened.

A strand of music floated through the air like a wisp of cobweb.

Drake stopped warming his hands.

Nell stopped shining her flashlight around.

Edgar stopped sighing.

Poe snored, moaning a wee bit.

And they all stared at each other (except Poe, who had his eyes closed).

"Great Scott!" whispered Drake.

"What *is* that?" whispered Nell.

"It's the ghosts," whispered Edgar. "They're singing."

Now, if one could have used a heart-o-matic meter at that moment, one would have seen three hearts hammering like crazy.

Edgar's heart was hammering especially hard. He wrung his hands, his face turned white as glue, and he moaned, "Oh, gloom and doom! Oh, spiders and bats! Now the ghosts are haunting us during the day, too!"

But Drake Doyle and Nell Fossey were science detective geniuses. And, like all science detective geniuses everywhere, they had a job to do, hammering hearts or not. They had no time to waste on gloom and doom.

Drake scribbled in his notebook, *ghost music, not bad, bebop maybe,* and then he drew a quick chart. (In a pinch, all good scientists draw charts.)

Meanwhile, Nell put her ear next to one of the open pipes. "Mr. Glum, where do these pipes go?"

"Oh, woe!" wailed Edgar. "I—I don't know where they go. I only live here!"

Nell frowned. "The music appears to be coming from these pipes."

"Curious." Drake knelt next to Nell. "Hello-oooooo. Aaaaaanybody theeeeeeere?" he called into one of the pipes.

And, just like that, the music stopped.

"Fascinating," said Drake.

"Eerily so," said Nell.

"See what I mean?" cried Edgar.

Nell cocked an eyebrow and looked at Drake. "Are you thinking what I'm thinking?" she asked.

Drake nodded. "At least I *think* I'm thinking what you're thinking."

"Well then," said Nell, sticking her pencil behind her ear, "I think we've seen enough." And up the stairs they went.

To everyone's surprise, Edgar's grandmother was standing at the top of the steps. She looked rather upset, as if she'd forgotten her name, or perhaps left her favorite book out in the rain. "They're here," she said.

"Who?" said Drake and Nell and Edgar together.

She lowered her voice to a whisper and glanced over her shoulder. "The ghosts. The ones Edgar's always talking about. I—I heard them."

Drake patted her hand. "Never fear, Grandmother Glum. We heard the ghosts, too."

Grandmother Glum gasped. "You—you did?"

"Indeed," said Nell, handing her a business card. "Only we have a hunch that it's not what you think."

"Now, without further ado," said Drake, "Scientist Nell and I must return to the lab."

"And then?" asked Edgar and Grandmother Glum together.

"Expect our report before nightfall," said Nell.

Edgar sighed sadly. "You probably won't call. No one ever does. And even if you do, it'll be too late."

And on that cheery note, out the door they went, blinking in the brilliant sunshine, leaving Edgar and his grandmother behind in the dark.

CHAPTER THREE
The Gory
Details

Back at the lab, Drake pulled a book off the shelf and thumbed through it to find the right section: "Haunted House Analysis: What to Do When Ghosts Moan, Play Bebop, or Just Clank Their Chains, and Everyone Is Quite Gloomy."

And while Drake and Nell read the section aloud, Drake's mom, Kate Doyle, stuck her head around the door. "Had breakfast yet?"

"Negative," they replied.

"How do cinnamon pancakes sound, with whipped cream and strawberries?"

"Make it so," said Drake.

"Like a dream," said Nell.

"Affirmative," replied Mrs. Doyle. "Hot chocolate anyone?"

"No, thanks," said Drake.

"Just coffee," said Nell. "Decaf. Black." (Real scientists don't drink hot chocolate. It makes them sleepy, and as everyone knows, it's more difficult to crack cases when one is sleepy.)

"Roger that," said Mrs. Doyle, and she was back in five minutes twenty-two seconds with coffee and breakfast. (Scientifically speaking, Mrs. Doyle was a whiz. You see, she owned her own catering company and so was quite used to whipping up specialties in nothing flat.)

So after saying "Thanks a billion!" to Mrs. Doyle, Drake and Nell washed their hands and sat at the lab table. They ate their breakfast and shared their observations. Then they developed a hypothesis. (Of course, as any scientist knows, a hypothesis is simply an educated guess.)

"Based upon our observations, Scientist Nell, I believe the haunting of Edgar's home is being caused by . . ."

Nell took a few notes, and nodded. "Agreed, Detective Doyle. Let's test our hypothesis."

So, for the rest of the morning, that's what they did. Using the latest in scientific gadgetry (their lab was filled with gadgets, compliments of Mr. Sam Doyle, who owned his own science equipment and supply company), they assembled a mini-simulation of what they believed was occurring at Edgar's home. After lunch (peanut butter and banana sandwiches with apple slices on the side), they tested the simulation.

"Ah-ha! Just as we thought," said Nell with a satisfied smile.

"Our hypothesis is correct," said Drake. And without wasting another second, he phoned Edgar. "Meet us in the lab, Mr. Glum. Bring Poe. Ten minutes and counting."

Nine minutes fifty-six seconds later, Edgar rushed into the lab with Poe at his heels. "Give me the gory details."

Drake sat on a stool with a drum in his lap. "Allow Scientist Nell to explain."

Nell clasped her hands behind her back and paced around the room. "Let us begin with a loud noise. Detective Doyle, if you would be so kind?"

"Certainly." Drake banged the drum with a drum stick. *BOOOOM!*

Nell stopped pacing and looked quite serious. "Did you hear that, Mr. Glum?"

Edgar frowned. "You'd have to be deaf not to hear that." (And indeed, Poe, being quite deaf, had settled into what looked to be a nice afternoon nap, completely undisturbed by all the ruckus.)

Nell continued, "Sound is caused by a vibrating object, in this case, a drum."

"You see," Drake explained, "the vibrating drum causes the molecules in the surrounding air to vibrate also, creating a sound wave that travels in all directions."

"And when that sound wave reaches your ear it signals your brain that you have heard a sound," finished Nell.

"But what does this have to do with ghosts and ghouls?" asked Edgar.

"Ah, yes," said Nell, stopping her pacing. "Now we've come to the heart of the matter. Imagine, if you will, a gigantic football stadium. Imagine the announcer calling the game play-by-play. Now I ask you, if you're sitting in the crowd, how are you able to hear the announcer?"

"But—but I've never been to a football game."

"Answer the question, Mr. Glum," said Drake.

Edgar crumpled and put his face in his hands. "I—I don't know!"

"It's because," said Nell, "the announcer's voice is *amplified.*"

Now it was Drake's turn to pace. "Amplification is when a sound is made louder. Even the shape of your own ears helps to amplify sound. Your outer ear funnels the sound into your ear canal, concentrating the sound. You can funnel even more sound by cupping your hands around your ears. Try it, and you will hear the difference."

And while Edgar cupped his ears, Drake placed a pipe next to Poe, who by this time was running in his sleep, moaning and howling a wee bit, while his license tags clinked and clanked. "Put your ear on the other end of this pipe, Mr. Glum."

Edgar listened through the pipe, and his mouth dropped open. "It's—it's my *ghost!* The howling, the moaning . . . it's him . . . it's *Poe.*"

"Quite right," said Drake. "We first became suspicious when you said that Poe stopped sleeping in your room on the *same* night the haunting started. And not only that—you had a new furnace."

Nell nodded. "A *warm* furnace, to be exact, one that burns wood—the perfect spot for sleeping if you're an old dog living in a chilly house."

"Very simply," said Drake, "Poe's moaning and howling, not to mention the sound of his license tags clinking together, were amplified through the pipes, which, no doubt, went all over the house, as old pipes often do."

"But what about the music we heard?"

"Elementary, really," said Drake. "It was simply your grandmother's radio being amplified to us in the basement. And when I hollered to ask if anyone was there, she heard *my* voice amplified, thought it was the ghost, and immediately turned off her radio to listen."

"It's all very logical once you think about it," said Nell. "Just plug up the pipes. Should take care of the problem."

"Thank you," Edgar said. "I'll tell my grandmother all about it." And suddenly, without any warning, rather like the sun bursting through fog, Edgar smiled and gave them each a hug. It was quite astonishing, scientifically speaking.

Later that evening, Drake wrote in his lab notebook:

Case solved.
Poe the sleepy culprit.
Invited Edgar to football game.
Received pet spider as payment.
(Gave to Nell, who named it "CREEPERS.")
Paid in full.

CHAPTER FOUR

Alien Invasion

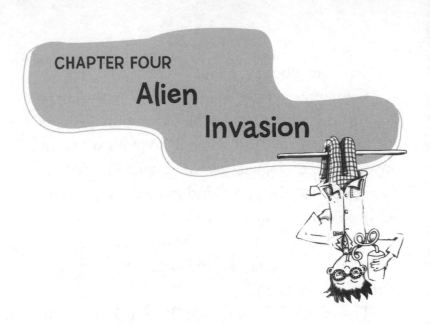

It was a splendid afternoon for hanging upside down while drinking a strawberry soda. In fact, Drake was doing just that when there was a *woof!* and a *scratch!* at the lab door. "Enter."

A dog nudged the door open with his snout.

"Ah, Dr. Livingston. *Slurp!* Ahhhh . . . Just checking the force of gravity versus the body's ability to keep things moving in the right direction. Now, come a little closer, my boy. That's it."

Drake reached into the pouch around the dog's neck and withdrew a note. On the outside, it read:

To: Detective Doyle
From: Naturalist Nell

Nell Fossey was not only a superb scientist, good with calculations and bubbling beakers, but she doubled as a naturalist. Simply put, Nell loved nature. Whether it was a sunset, a buffalo, or a clam, Nell was fascinated.

Drake opened the note.

Dear Detective Doyle,
It was good of you to come over yesterday. At least there was some sunshine once it stopped raining.

Last night I watched the movie Psycho Alien Invasion! I'm heading over to Mossy Lake University later to see my mother; hope my bike doesn't get swamped in the mud. —Naturalist Nell

An ordinary-sounding note. Nell's mother taught wildlife biology at Mossy Lake University. It was only natural that Nell would want to visit Professor Fossey. And Drake knew that *Psycho Alien Invasion!* was a pretty good movie—he'd seen it eleven times and counting. But, mothers and movies aside, Drake knew that this was no ordinary note. No, indeed. Drake knew it was a secret code for something else entirely. . . .

"Dr. Livingston, would you be so kind as to fetch my secret code card from my desk? Yes, that's it . . . a little to the left . . . No, no, not my *Flying Saucer Identification Guide* . . . it's right under your nose, that's it . . . bring it here." And giving Dr. Livingston a pat, Drake took his secret code card and held it over the note (while taking a sip of strawberry soda). The secret message appeared.

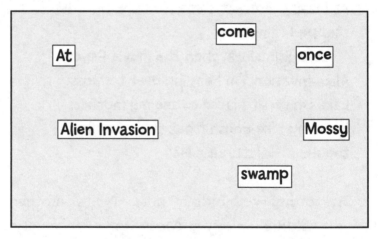

Alien Invasion! Drake was so shocked that for a moment the forces of gravity got the better of him. With a *burp!* and a *fizz!* strawberry soda bubbled out of his nose.

"Great Scott!" cried Drake, falling to the floor in a heap. "Aliens have invaded Mossy Swamp!"

Woof! Woof! cried Dr. Livingston.

"Naturalist Nell could be in dire danger. Quick! To Mossy Swamp we go!"

Drake raced his bike over High Hill, around Lonely Loop, past Plum Pond toward Mossy Swamp, while Dr. Livingston ran alongside.

Mossy Swamp was a wetland filled with wild-flowers, grasses, frogs, snakes, bogs, and bugs. To think that aliens had invaded it was almost more than he could bear. Perhaps even now the purple-headed, bloodsucking Martians were ripping the legs off frogs, smashing bugs under their scaly feet, and—horrors of horrors!—plowing the swamp under to make a landing pad for their flying saucers!

"Halloooo! Naturalist Nell! Yoo-hoo!" Drake cried upon arriving at the swamp, quite breathless.

Much to his relief, Nell popped up from the undergrowth. Except for a few twigs in her hair she looked okay. "Ah, there you are. Just preparing for our field trip tomorrow with the first graders."

Taking no chances, Drake whipped out his *Super-Alien-Stunner-Shocker-Whammy* from his backpack (guaranteed to stun any bloodsucking Martian for sixty seconds or your money back). "Never fear, Naturalist Nell, Drake Doyle is here!"

"Uh—thank you, Detective Doyle, but I don't think you'll be needing that."

"But—but your note said there was an alien—"

"Indeed there is an alien invasion. But it's not what you think." Nell pointed at a tall plant with purple blossoms (quite pretty, in Drake's opinion). "Observe, the alien species."

"Huh?"

"Purple loosegoose, a noxious weed. Not all aliens come from outer space, you know."

In the space of a nanosecond (one one-zillionth of the time it takes to blink), Drake Doyle overcame his disappointment. And though battling purple-headed weeds was not nearly as exciting as battling purple-headed bloodsucking Martians, an alien was an alien. He hastily put away his *Super-Alien-Stunner-Shocker-Whammy*, whipped open his notebook, grabbed his pencil from behind his ear and said, "Take it from the top."

Nell paced, her hands clasped behind her back. "You see, it's all about ecosystems."

"Ah yes, ecosystems—the balance of nature."

"When a large number of plants and animals live together successfully for a long period of time, the ecosystem is said to be *balanced*. But when something happens, say a drought or disease—"

24

"—or a new strip mall perhaps?"

"Precisely—then the ecosystem becomes *out of balance* and many plants or animals may die."

"Tragic."

"And as you know, Detective Doyle, Mossy Swamp is a wetland. And wetlands are part of a vast ecosystem, with everything interconnected. The animals and bugs have what they need to live and reproduce, and likewise the plants."

Drake was scribbling furiously. "Uh-huh, yes, I see . . . fascinating, really . . ."

"Now, noxious weeds are plants that *do not belong* in an ecosystem. In other words, they are alien invaders. Case in point, purple loosegoose."

"Did it arrive by spaceship perhaps?"

"Negative, Detective Doyle."

"Let me guess, Naturalist Nell. Did it arrive as a seed, carried by a bird through its droppings?"

"Happens all the time."

"Or perhaps carried on the wind from someone's backyard—someone who didn't know that purple loosegoose is a noxious weed and planted it simply because it was pretty?"

"Again, correct." Suddenly, with no warning, Nell grabbed the purple loosegoose, and with an "Arrgggh!" ripped it up by the roots.

Drake stared at her, his mouth hanging open. He dropped his pencil into the muck. (Normally his partner was quite even-tempered, so this exhibit of raw animalism was extraordinary.)

"Unless we stop the purple loosegoose," she was saying, "it will take over Mossy Swamp!"

"Good heavens!" cried Drake. "Are you certain? I mean—it *does* look fairly harm—"

"I'm quite certain." Nell stuffed the purple loosegoose into her backpack. "Come, Detective Doyle. Let us proceed to Nature Headquarters immediately, and I'll show you what I mean."

CHAPTER FIVE

A Pleasant Outing?

Vines snaked everywhere. Gigantic leaves glittered, and papier-mâché trees soared overhead. Indeed, if you didn't wander too far, you might think you were deep in a jungle. But it was really just Nature Headquarters, AKA Nell's bedroom.

Mixed in among the smells of rabbit fuzz and frog water, were squeaks, screeches, squawks, and, if you listened closely, a little snoring as well.

Nell placed the purple loosegoose onto a shelf for later classification, and sat at her desk with Drake. "Observe," she said, clicking the computer mouse. "This video scene was taken last year in a wetland much like Mossy Swamp."

Together they watched a most horrible scene unfold. At first the wetland looked quite cheerful. Birds chirped. Snakes slithered. Frogs hopped. Butterflies flitted among the grasses and wildflowers.

Drake pushed up his glasses. "Say, isn't that a cluster of purple—"

"Sharp eye, Detective. Indeed, it is our alien invader, purple loosegoose. Now observe. . . ."

A troop of Boy Scouts appeared on the screen. They trooped merrily along the wetland path, stopping for photo ops, or to sniff the flowers. All in all, it looked like a pleasant outing.

But Drake was disturbed. Something wasn't quite right. "Say, isn't the purple loosegoose growing? I mean—*fast?*"

Sure enough, in the time it takes to say "Bob's Your Uncle," the purple loosegoose overwhelmed the path. There was a flash of purple, an arm here and a leg there, then the troop of Boy Scouts disappeared in a tangle of beautiful purple blossoms, to the tune of *"Help! Help!"*

And then the video abruptly ended.

Drake jumped up. "Jeepers creepers!"

"Jeepers creepers is right," said Nell. "Once purple loosegoose reaches a certain stage in its life cycle, it grows out of control. Eventually it takes over entire wetlands, muscling out other plants and leaving little food for the bugs and animals that live there. The ecosystem collapses and most species die."

"Great Scott! Purple loosegoose is *worse* than a purple-headed bloodsucking Martian!" cried Drake.

Nell's mouth formed a thin line. "Brace yourself, Detective Doyle. It gets worse."

"Worse? How could it get any worse?!"

"Have you forgotten? Tomorrow is the annual first-grade field trip to the wetlands. And *we're* the guest lecturers."

Drake gulped. Nell was right. This was worse.

Nell tapped her watch. "And, by my estimation, tomorrow is the day all the purple loosegoose let loose and grow like mad."

Suddenly, Drake felt faint. "Egads! We could all be swallowed alive! What on earth shall we do?"

"That's the thing, Drake," Nell said. "I just don't know what to do. Cancel the field trip, I suppose, and close the wetland to the public. Not very scientific. And while it may save the first graders, it certainly won't save the wetland."

"My, my," said Drake. "This is dire. Quite dire. There, there. Chin up, Naturalist Nell. Dire as it may be, we must find a solution."

And so, as all scientists do when stumped, they brainstormed. They brainstormed and brainstormed, talking louder and louder until they were shouting. Now, you might think they were desperate, or mad at each other perhaps, but they were shouting for a different reason altogether. You see, it was becoming difficult to hear because the noise in the jungle was growing louder by the second. Not squeaks, screeches, squawks or a little snoring, mind you, but a steady *chomp! Chomp! CHOMP! CHOMP!*

The *chomp! Chomp! CHOMP! CHOMP!* grew louder and louder until Nell finally screamed, "WHO'S MAKING ALL THAT RACKET?" The noise stopped. Then there was a little burp.

Drake and Nell glanced in the direction of the burp. Right where Nell had placed the purple loosegoose were nine fat beetles. The purple loosegoose was gone. One of the bugs patted its belly, sighed, and burped a bug-sized *buuuurrrrp!*

Drake pushed up his glasses. "You don't suppose . . ."

Nell blinked. "This is amazing . . ."

"The beetles ate the loosegoose!" cried Drake.

"Fascinating. My mother gave me the beetles for my birthday. Scientific name: *Chompicus*

cinderellus. Picky eaters. So far all they've eaten is spinach. I worried that I'd have to return them to the wetlands where my mother first classified them. They've been moping around for weeks. Hungry, no doubt."

"Hungry for purple loosegoose," said Drake.

Nell cocked her eyebrow. "Are you thinking what I'm thinking, Detective Doyle?"

"Indeed I am. There's no time to lose."

"Check."

So, after gathering the beetles they were off.

Back at the swamp, Nell released the beetles. Soon there was a *chomp*. . . .

Which grew to a *Chomp!* And then a *CHOMP!* And finally, a satisfying, *CHOMP! CHOMP! CHOMP!*

The next morning, the wetland looked quite cheerful. Birds chirped. Snakes slithered. Frogs hopped. Butterflies flitted among the grasses and wildflowers.

A group of first graders appeared on the scene. They trooped along the wetland path, whistling merrily, some stopping for photo ops, some stooping to sniff the flowers. Meanwhile Nell Fossey chatted about ecosystems, before inviting Drake Doyle to chat a bit about alien invasions. All in all, it was a pleasant outing.

Later that day, Drake wrote in his lab notebook:

> Aliens destroyed.
> Beetles superheroes (and super fat).
> Professor Fossey says we're onto something here.
> Received immense satisfaction for a job well done.
> Paid in full.

CHAPTER SIX

Step
Right Up!

Nell was just tossing a couple of *Bert's Best Bug Bon-Bons* to her lizards when the phone rang.

"Doyle and Fossey," she answered.

"WHAT?" hollered a voice amid lots of background noise. "I CAN'T HEAR YOU!"

And Nell, understanding that a customer was in desperate need of proper communication, shouted, "DOYLE AND FOSSEY!!!"

"OH, NELL, THANK GOODNESS YOU'RE THERE! IT'S ME—JUNE JEWELL. I COULD REALLY USE YOUR HELP!"

June Jewell was in Drake and Nell's class at school. June was a nice girl, although, sadly, her life was not always easy. As everyone knew, June's large family struggled to make ends meet, as many large families often do. Sometimes June came to class without any mittens, or with shoes that weren't her size or perhaps with a rock for show-and-tell.

"OF COURSE, MS. JEWELL. 'HELP' IS OUR MIDDLE NAME."

"*WHAT'S* YOUR MIDDLE NAME?"

"NEVER MIND. WHAT SEEMS TO BE THE PROBLEM?" Already the case was proving to be quite difficult. But Nell was up to the challenge. She whipped her pencil from behind her ear.

"I'M AT THE CARNIVAL," shouted June.

Every year the carnival came to town. Kids from all over flocked there to win prizes, ride rides, and eat themselves silly.

"DID YOU EAT YOURSELF SILLY, MS. JEWELL? ARE YOU SICK? DO YOU REQUIRE EMERGENCY MEASURES?"

"WELL, I'M HEARTSICK. DOES THAT COUNT?"

Heartsick! Nell was so dismayed she almost fell off her chair. Being sick at heart (sad, lonely, forlorn, weepy, forsaken, miserable, low . . .) was far, far worse than a tummy-ache. It lasted far longer and hurt just as much, maybe worse.

"MY BROTHERS AND SISTERS ARE, TOO!"

Now Nell *did* fall off her chair. This was heart-sickness times twelve, for June had eleven brothers and sisters. "YOU—YOU MEAN—"

"THAT'S RIGHT. JOE, JAY, JOY, JOAN, JOHN, JEAN, JANE, JENN, JEB, JED, AND LITTLE JUDD JUNIOR, TOO."

"WE'LL BE RIGHT THERE. LIKE I SAID, 'HELP' IS OUR MIDDLE NAME!"

"*WHAT'S* YOUR MIDDLE NAME?"

"OH—NEVER MIND. JUST TELL US WHERE TO MEET YOU. . . ."

Nell hung up and called Drake. "CARNIVAL ENTRANCE ASAP!"

"CHECK! UH—NELL, WHY ARE WE YELLING?"

"Oh, sorry."

"No harm done."

"Carnival. Ten minutes and counting."

"Check."

Click.

The smell of corn dogs and cotton candy filled the air. There were balloons and merry-go-rounds and bumper cars, laughter and music. "You see, it's like this," June explained once Drake and Nell entered the carnival. "Grams and Gramps came to visit us and gave me—I—I mean gave *each of us*—five dollars."

Drake whipped out his notebook. "Let's see, five times twelve . . ."

"Where are your brothers and sisters?" asked Nell.

"They're over at Shady Jim's booth. He's giving away a free, all-expenses paid trip for the whole family to Magic Valley's Fabulous Fun-O-Rama if anyone can win his game. The only problem is—"

"Yes?" Drake and Nell said together.

"We keep losing." June pulled two very crumpled dollar bills from her pocket.

"This is all we have left."

"Great Scott!" cried Drake. "According to my calculations, that's a loss of fifty-eight dollars!"

"That's why I'm so heartsick," said June. "We've never taken a vacation. There are just too many of us. The farthest I've ever been from home is, uh—well, right here at the carnival."

"I see," said Nell. "Well, much as we want to help your family go on a nice vacation, I'm afraid we can't help you win. That would be cheating—"

And all might have ended right there, had

June not grabbed Nell's sleeve and begged, "But Shady Jim wins every time! It looks so *easy* when he does it. That's why I called you."

"Hmm," said Nell. "Sounds suspicious."

"Suspicious indeed," said Drake, pushing up his glasses. "Let's check it out. Ms. Jewell, lead the way, if you please."

Soon they reached Shady Jim's booth, surrounded by a crowd of children, including Joe, Jay, Joy, Joan, John, Jean, Jane, Jenn, Jeb, Jed, and little Judd Junior, all of whom looked terribly sad. "STEP RIGHT UP," Shady Jim hollered, "don't be shy! Winning this game's as easy as pie!"

And to show just how easy the game was to win, Shady Jim demonstrated. "Ever play air hockey, kiddos? It's kind of like that. Stand at one end of the alley, and aim for the target at the other end." And while everyone watched, Shady Jim aimed the puck, and gave it a push. The puck sailed across the smooth surface until it stopped dead center in the bull's-eye.

"Oooh, aaaah!" exclaimed the crowd.

And for good measure, Shady Jim did the same thing again and again and again and *again*. (He even did it blindfolded, and once while doing jumping jacks, and backwards. Scientifically speaking, it was amazing.) "See, kiddos? What'd I tell you?" gloated Shady Jim. "Easy as pie. Keep winning and you keep playing. Hit the bull's-eye five times in a row, and your family will win a one-week trip to Magic Valley's Fabulous Fun-O-Rama, all expenses paid. Now who's it gonna be? Step right up and try your luck!"

Money was flying everywhere, so fast Shady Jim could hardly stuff his pockets quickly enough. And, while Drake, Nell, and June watched, kid after kid played the game. A few made the bull's-eye. Most didn't. And those who did happen to land the puck into the target rarely did it twice in a row. Certainly not three times in a row. Four times was out of the question. And five times seemed quite impossible indeed.

"Too bad, kid," Shady Jim would say. "NEXT!"

"Hmm," said Nell, punching the numbers into her calculator. "Something's not adding up."

"See?" said June, her lip quivering. "It's hopeless. How can I possibly win? Mom, Dad, Joe, Jay, Joy, Joan, John, Jean, Jane, Jenn, Jeb, Jed, and little Judd Junior will be so disappointed."

And as June pulled out an old cloth and dabbed her eyes, there arose a rumpus around the booth.

"We have a WINNER!" Shady Jim hollered.

CHAPTER SEVEN
The Winner!

June gasped.

Drake broke the lead in his pencil.

Nell hit the wrong calculator button.

"It's Baloney!" they all cried. "He won!"

(Now, in case you didn't know, Baloney's real name was Bubba Mahoney, but when he was a toddler he ate seven and a half packages of baloney in one sitting, and so then everyone called him Baloney. It made sense.) Baloney was the biggest kid in the fifth grade, good for stomping aluminum pop cans, driving in nails with his fists, and sitting on things if he felt they needed squishing.

Baloney danced about. "I won! I won!"

Shady Jim grinned. "See, kids? If Baloney can win, *anyone* can win!"

"Egads!" gasped Drake. "If Baloney's here—"

"—that means Frisco can't be far!" cried Nell.

You see, Baloney and James Frisco, the ~~bad~~ mad scientist, were partners. If Frisco needed anything squished, Baloney was his man. If Baloney needed anything blown up, Frisco was his man.

"Do you suppose Frisco, Baloney, and Shady Jim are all in it together?" asked Drake.

June gasped. "But that would be cheating!"

"Cheating indeed, Ms. Jewell," agreed Nell. "But it's all we've got to go on right now."

"Great Scott!" cried Drake, ducking behind June. "Don't look now. To your left. By the corn dogs. Under the tree. James Frisco! The very man!"

Sure enough, there was James Frisco, the ~~bad~~ mad scientist. He gazed at the sky, whistling like he didn't have a care in the world.

"Do you think he's seen us?" asked Nell while, fast as a proton, she ducked behind June as well.

"Negative," replied Drake. "His powers of observation are quite terrible, as you know."

"This could be our big break," said Nell.

"We must spring into action," said Drake.

They opened their detective kits. They whipped out their magnifying glasses. They whipped out their periscopes. Their binoculars. Their insect repellent (it *was* a rather buggy day). And with June as their cover, they began to do surveillance (to stake out, observe, shadow), determined to expose Frisco, the ~~bad~~ mad scientist, at his game.

"Subject is eyeing the corn dogs," observed Drake.

"Subject is—*eeww*—picking his nose," observed Nell.

"Subject appears quite overheated," observed Drake.

"A warm day to be dressed in an overcoat," added Nell.

"Subject is whistling out of tune," said Drake.

"Subject also putting his hand in his pocket frequently," said Nell.

"Hmm . . . let me adjust my binoculars . . . Great Scott!" cried Drake. "You're right, Scientist Nell. And—Great Scott times two!—there are wires coming out of his pocket!"

"Good eye, Detective Doyle. Now just where do you suppose those wires lead?"

Peering through their binoculars, they saw that the wires trailed across the ground, disappearing beneath . . .

Both Drake and Nell gasped and said, "Beneath Shady Jim's booth!"

Drake, Nell, and June darted behind the back of the booth where the wires disappeared.

"Quick, Scientist Nell, my periscope!"

"Check!"

Drake slipped the periscope under the booth and peered into the scope. (In actual fact, Drake first removed a pebble that was stuck in his knee, bumped his nose against the wall of the booth—"Ow!"—and *then* slipped the periscope under the booth for a quick peek around.)

"Report?" asked Nell.

"There are many hairy legs crawling around, it's just horrible . . . oh, oh, wait a minute. Bug on my periscope. Off you go . . . Ah, yes. That's better. Fascinating. Quite fascinating."

"Report?"

"One of the wires is hooked to the positive terminal of a large battery. The other wire is coiled around what looks to be an enormous nail, before being hooked to the negative terminal. Quick, Scientist Nell, hand me a paper clip."

"Check."

And, being the best partner a scientist could have, Nell whipped out a paper clip. (Where did she get it, you wonder? Wonder no longer, for both Drake and Nell's detective kits were chock

full of handy gadgets. You see, science detectives must be prepared for every possibility—such as desperate customers, suspicious characters, even the occasional earthquake.) But before Nell could hand the paper clip to Drake, something extraordinary happened.

Just as Shady Jim began once again to demonstrate his easy-as-pie game, the paper clip flew out of Nell's hand as if by magic, and disappeared quick as a quark beneath the booth.

"Well," whispered Drake, rather stunned. "I think that answers that."

"Indeed," replied Nell. She cocked her eyebrow, which always meant she was quite serious. "Are you thinking what I'm thinking?"

"Indeed I am, Scientist Nell."

"You'll need wire cutters, I presume?" Nell was already rummaging through her detective kit.

"Check."

She handed the wire cutters to Drake, who disappeared under the booth.

"Wait for my signal, Detective Doyle." Without wasting a second, Nell turned to June. "Ms. Jewell? I believe it is time for you to win that trip to Magic Valley's Fabulous Fun-O-Rama."

CHAPTER EIGHT
Fun-O-Wama

"Lookee here!" hollered Shady Jim as he snatched June's last two crumpled dollars. "The little lady wants to try her luck once again. Millionth time's a charm, I always say."

Joe, Jay, Joy, Joan, John, Jean, Jane, Jenn, Jeb, Jed, and little Judd Junior crowded around June.

"C'mon, Sis, you can do it, we know you can."

"Win for the family."

June placed her hands on the puck, took a deep breath, and looked at Nell.

Nell nodded, then yelled, "THREE, TWO, ONE . . . GO!"

June pushed the puck.

The crowd leaned forward, watching, as the puck sailed across the surface. Four feet . . . eight feet . . . twelve feet . . . and then . . . *BULL'S-EYE!*

There was some polite cheering. June's brothers and sisters looked just a tad less heartsick.

Shady Jim laughed. "Har! Har! Well, kiddos, hitting the bull's-eye once is a breeze, but can she do it twice in a row? Go ahead, little lady."

Again June pushed the puck. And again June made a bull's-eye. Now Shady Jim looked a little nervous. The crowd cheered again. In the distance, Nell saw Frisco frowning, his hand jammed in his pocket, looking like a ~~bad~~ mad scientist whose experiment had gone suddenly, horribly wrong.

For indeed . . . *it had.*

June hit the bull's-eye not only twice, but three times, four times, and five. By the time she hit the fifth bull's-eye, the crowd was going wild. Joe, Jay, Joy, Joan, John, Jean, Jane, Jenn, Jeb, Jed, and little Judd Junior were leaping with glee and doing cartwheels. "Fun-O-Rama, here we come!"

Drake joined Nell, and shook her hand. "Bravo as usual, Scientist Nell."

"Ditto, Detective Doyle."

And while more and more children gave Shady Jim their two dollars, each winning a trip to Magic Valley's Fabulous Fun-O-Rama, June's brothers and sisters gathered around Nell and

Drake. "How did you do it?" asked June. "How did you beat them at their game?"

"Elementary," replied Drake. "Allow Scientist Nell to explain."

"Thank you, Detective Doyle." Nell paced the grass, hands clasped behind her back. "Chances are, every one of you has at one time or another played with a magnet."

"Not me," said little Judd Junior. "I've only pwayed with wocks." ("Pwayed with wocks" = "played with rocks" in Little Judd Junior Language.)

Nell continued, "Well, little Judd Junior, you will be happy to know that a magnet is a particular *kind* of rock, a rock that has a *magnetic field*."

"Oh, boy," said little Judd Junior, "'cause I wike wocks."

"You see," added Drake. "A magnetic field is similar to an electrical current. In a magnet, the magnetic field flows from its north pole to its south pole—"

"North pole?" asked June.

"Not the kind with Santa Claus," Nell said.

"I wike Santa Cwaus a wot," whispered little Judd Junior. "He always bwings me wocks."

Nell paced some more. "You see, magnets

always have a north and south pole. Divide a magnet in half, and you now have two magnets, each with its own north and south pole. Quite amazing, really."

"I wish *I* had a magnet," said little Judd Junior.

"Ah," said Nell. "The good news, little Judd Junior, is that some magnets occur naturally. You can find them in the ground."

Little Judd Junior smiled. "Weawy?"

"Yes, but naturally occurring magnets are usually quite weak. Stronger magnets, however, can be created using an ordinary piece of metal and electricity. Detective Doyle?"

"Thank you, Scientist Nell." Drake took off his glasses and polished them before slipping them back on. "You can build your own magnet with a battery, some wire, and a nail."

"Yay!" Little Judd Junior hopped up and down.

Drake continued. "Hook one end of the wire to the positive terminal of the battery, wrap it around the nail, then hook the other end of the wire to the negative terminal, and *voila!* You have turned a normal, everyday nail into—"

"—an electromagnet," said Nell. "And just like any magnet, the nail now has a north pole and a south pole, or what we scientists would call a positive and a negative pole."

"But, *unlike* a regular magnet," said Drake, "an electromagnet can be turned off simply by disconnecting it from the battery."

"But," asked June, a little confused, "what does this have to do with Shady Jim, and the bull's-eye?"

"Ah, Ms. Jewell," said Drake, "now we come to the heart of the matter. As you may well know, opposites attract. The south pole of one magnet will attract the north pole of another magnet, and they will stick together like glue. So how did Shady Jim do it? You see, *the puck was also a magnet.*"

June, Joe, Jay, Joy, Joan, John, Jean, Jane, Jenn, Jeb, Jed, and little Judd Junior gasped. "But that's cheating!"

"Whenever Shady Jim played the game," said Nell, "the electromagnet was activated—"

"By Frisco," added Drake.

Nell continued, "—and the puck went straight to the bull's-eye because underneath the bull's-eye was the powerful electromagnet. The two opposite poles of the two magnets were attracted to each other. Shady Jim could never miss."

"But," said Drake, "whenever one of *you* tried to win, Frisco simply shut off the electromagnet, making it very difficult to land the puck on the bull's-eye."

"But how did he shut it off?" asked June.

"Excellent question, Ms. Jewell," replied Nell. "No doubt Frisco had a switch in his pocket. Whenever the switch was on, the electrical circuit was complete and the magnet was active. Whenever the switch was off, the circuit was broken and the magnet was off. All Drake did was snip the wire leading to Frisco's pocket and attach it to the battery, making a new circuit."

"Right again, Scientist Nell," said Drake. "The new circuit turned the magnet on permanently, regardless of whether Frisco's switch was on or off. Then, like Shady Jim, June could not lose."

"That's our Sis," said Joe, Jay, Joy, Joan, John, Jean, Jane, Jenn, Jeb, Jed, and little Judd Junior.

"Thanks, Drake and Nell," said June. "I'll bring you each a T-shirt from Magic Valley's Fabulous Fun-O-Rama as payment."

Drake and Nell shook hands all around, and left the carnival. (But not before stocking up on some essential supplies: cotton candy, licorice ropes, and a few candy apples. After all, scientists must be prepared for every possibility. . . .)

CHAPTER NINE
Danger in the Air

On this particular blustery morning, Drake was up to his ears in an important experiment. Highly important. He poured a brown solution into a yellow solution, added a pinch of *Smell So Squishy*, plus a smidge of *WOWza!* and swirled it around.

"Ahh," he said as a fragrance filled the room. He recorded the results in his lab notebook:

> Banana perfume just right.
> Must dab behind ears and monitor.

As he was dabbing, the phone rang. "Doyle and Fossey," answered Drake.

It was Nell. "Drake, have you forgotten?"

"Forgotten what?"

"You were supposed to meet me to ride our

bikes over to Peabody Park. We were going to practice our speeches to get ready for the Mossy Lake Days Parade at two o'clock, remember?"

The Mossy Lake Days Parade was in honor of the town's 100th birthday. The parade would begin at the school, march down Main Street, and wind through town, over the river and through the woods, ending at Peabody Park, where there would be a splendid picnic for all. Besides live music and a speech from the mayor, there would be speeches from Drake and Nell, dressed as Horace Peabody and Polly Plum, Mossy Lake's first pioneers, who happened also to be top-notch scientists. (Dr. Horace Peabody invented the flying kazoo, while Polly Plum was famous for her research on the dining habits of barn owls.)

"Great Scott!" cried Drake, accidentally spilling banana perfume on his lab coat. "I completely forgot! Give me ten minutes."

"Wear your rain gear. Nasty weather."

"Check."

Click.

Nell and Dr. Livingston were waiting at the corner by the time Drake arrived. Nell held onto her rain hat to keep it from blowing away.

"My apologies," Drake gasped, quite worn out from riding his bike into the wind.

"No problem. Did you bring your speech?"

"Affirmative. Written on water-repellent paper with smudge-proof ink. Invented it myself."

Just then a gust of wind swirled past Nell, and she looked a bit puzzled. "That's odd."

"What's odd?"

"Suddenly I smell bananas."

And with that, they were off, pedaling down Main Street, with Dr. Livingston running alongside.

Until recently, if one wanted to get to Peabody Park, one had to wind all the way through Porcupine Loop, past Unfortunate Bend, across Plum River, and then pedal (or drive) over Mole Hill before finally ending up at the park. But, to the delight of all, a new bridge had just been constructed over Plum River, connecting Peabody Park directly to town.

The new Mossy Lake Bridge was lovely to look at, with cables, arches, and sidewalks, plus a splendid view over the gorge and Plum River.

Drake and Nell were pedaling too fast to admire the view. They were halfway across the bridge when it happened.

The bridge moved. Not much, just a teensy bit (rather as if they'd hit a bump in the road), but indeed, it moved.

Drake and Nell screeched to a stop.

And through the wind and rain, the two scientists stared at each other.

"Did you feel that, Detective Doyle?"

"Indeed I did, Scientist Nell."

And, just in case they hadn't *really* felt it the first time, the wind gusted. There was another *bump!* and then a little *heave!* and maybe a *sigh!*

"Oh, my," said Nell.

"This isn't good," said Drake.

Woof! cried Dr. Livingston.

"I have a bad, bad feeling about this." Nell peered over the edge into the gorge and the raging river below. "There's danger in the air and it smells like bananas."

"Hmm. What do you think we should do?"

Nell looked at Drake. Her mouth formed a firm line, and Drake knew she meant business. "In just a few hours there will be a lot of people on the bridge: bands, cheerleaders, floats, horses, and trucks. If the bridge isn't safe . . ." She left the rest unsaid, because the possibilities were just too horrible to imagine, much less say aloud.

Drake shuddered. "Agreed. We must return to the lab for analysis immediately to determine why the bridge is moving. After all, public safety is more important than polished speeches."

So as the bridge sighed again, groaning and hiccupping, Drake and Nell hurried back to the lab, with Dr. Livingston leading the way.

There was indeed danger in the air, and it smelled like bananas.

CHAPTER TEN
Bridge Gone Bananas

Mrs. Doyle poked her head around the lab door. "Hmm . . . I thought you two were at Peabody Park practicing your speeches."

"Pressing business," said Nell.

"Public safety is our priority," said Drake.

"Lunch, anyone? Vegetarian chili perhaps? Cheese and crackers? And how about some dill pickles and bana—" Mrs. Doyle sniffed the air. "Oh, smells like you've already raided the banana bunch."

"Excellent menu options," replied Drake.

"Count me in," added Nell.

"Got it," said Mrs. Doyle. "Back in five."

Drake pulled a book off the shelf, turning to the section titled: "Danger in the Air: What to

Do When Your Bridge Sighs, Hiccups, Heaves, and Otherwise Goes Bananas." Drake and Nell read the section together, their expressions grim.

Mrs. Doyle returned with lunch. "Now don't forget the parade starts at two."

Drake glanced at his watch. "T minus one hundred eight minutes, and counting."

"Horace Peabody and Polly Plum won't let Mossy Lake down," said Nell, taking a sip of coffee.

After eating lunch, Drake and Nell sprang into action. They developed a hypothesis, as all good scientists do. They built simulations and tested their hypothesis. They checked the weather report, and then discovered a most spectacular, most terrifying video on the Internet. . . .

Dr. Livingston whined and covered his eyes with his paws, unable to watch a second more.

"Horrifying," said Drake, quite aghast.

"Mortifying," agreed Nell, no less aghast.

Drake checked his watch. "Great Scott! It's T minus three!"

"Roger that, Detective Doyle. I'm on it!"

Woof! Woof!

"Quick, Mom!" cried Drake down the attic stairs. "My costume!"

"Quick, Mom!" cried Nell over the phone. "My costume!"

Meanwhile, at the school parking lot where the parade had gathered, the mood was gloomy.

First of all, it was raining. Second, the wind was picking up. (The clowns had to hold their wigs on their heads with both hands, and the princesses were quite nervous about losing their tiaras.) Third, and perhaps worst of all, the leaders of the parade were, well, . . . *missing.*

The mayor paced this way and that.

The band played "America the Beautiful" to pass the time.

Finally, at five minutes past T minus zero (2:05 P.M.), they could wait no longer.

The mayor said, "The parade must go on!"

So, following a siren blast from the fire engine truck, the parade began marching down Main Street, flanked by the crowd, who cheered in spite of the rain. The cheerleaders waved soggy pom-poms. The band played the Mossy Lake theme song. Princesses tossed candy from floats.

Down Main Street they marched, past Barko's Supermart and Iggy's Ice Cream Parlor, toward Mossy Lake Bridge (which was, thankfully, empty of people because there was no room for both the parade *and* the spectators).

Then, just as the parade reached the bridge, who should come screeching to a halt on their bicycles but Horace Peabody and Polly Plum (otherwise known as Drake Doyle and Nell Fossey in costume), plus Dr. Livingston.

"Stop the parade!" cried Peabody and Plum.

Woof! cried Dr. Livingston.

The parade came to a screeching halt. (The band bumped into the mayor. *Oompa!* The cheerleaders bumped into the band. *Ow!* The princess float bumped into the fire engine. *Ouooga!* The clowns bumped into the princess float. *Oof!*)

"Sorry to rain on your parade," Plum said through her megaphone.

"But we have a situation," said Peabody through his megaphone.

"Hush! Shh!" people were saying. "The town's founders are speaking!"

"Riding our bikes on our way to Peabody Park this morning," said Plum, "we became aware of a great danger."

"We were in the middle of the bridge," said Peabody, "when it moved."

"It heaved and sighed," said Plum. "And our

sixth scientific sense kicked into gear. Something was wrong. Terribly, terribly wrong."

"But what could be wrong?" asked the tuba player. "We just built the bridge. Looks fine to me."

Everyone looked at the bridge. And indeed, except for being wet, it looked fine and dandy.

Just then, the bridge swayed ever so slightly and then did a little shiver.

The crowd gasped.

"It's called resonance," said Plum. She got off her bicycle and paced in front of the bridge. "You see, every object has a natural vibration."

"Quite right, Professor Plum," remarked Peabody, getting off his bike as well. "Look around you. Everything you see in nature, in the universe, vibrates. From atoms and molecules—"

"—to bridges, the Eiffel Tower, and trees—" added Plum.

"—everything moves with its own natural vibration," continued Peabody. "Hard to believe, I know, but it's true."

"Now," said Plum, looking quite serious, "you can enhance an object's natural vibration by adding more vibration at the same frequency. Case in point: sing in the shower, and notice that there is one pitch in particular that sounds especially wonderful. That one pitch is the natural vibration, or frequency, of the room. Adding your voice at the same vibration creates even more vibration. This is called resonance, or sympathetic vibration."

Plum indicated the bridge behind her, which, at that very moment, hiccupped. "This bridge has a natural frequency. If the wind matches that natural frequency, like singing in the shower, the vibrations can become more pronounced."

Peabody said, "On a windy day in 1940, the Tacoma Narrows Bridge, nicknamed 'Galloping Gertie,' galloped so hard that the sidewalk on the right lurched up to be 28 feet higher than the sidewalk on the left before it plunged the other way."

"Quite astonishing, really," said Plum. "We saw the video ourselves. There were people on the bridge. They had to get out of their cars and crawl to safety."

"Naturally," said Peabody, "the bridge could only take so much. It broke apart and plunged into the water below."

"Look!" A clown pointed at the bridge.

Just then the wind howled and the bridge swayed again. It moaned. It groaned. And then it began to buck like a mule.

The crowd gasped. "It's going bananas!"

Indeed, the bridge *had gone bananas*. It galloped. It swayed. It bucked and kicked. It creaked. It moaned and hollered. And while the entire town of Mossy Lake watched, horrified, it broke apart, and disappeared into the gorge below.

There followed a moment of deep silence. Dr. Peabody and Professor Plum, and everyone in Mossy Lake for that matter, were quite stunned.

"Well—uh . . ." began the mayor in a wobbly voice. "I think I can speak for all of us when I say that, once again, the founders of Mossy Lake are our heroes. You've saved countless lives. Thank you, Professor Plum and Dr. Peabody. Strangely enough, this whole incident has made me hungry for bananas!" And he shook their hands while cameras flashed. The crowd cheered wildly.

That evening, Drake wrote in his notebook:

Town SAVED.
Bridge to be re-engineered.
Nell and I named town's
honorary heroes.
Given picnic in honor, with banana
pudding for dessert.
Thoroughly sick of bananas. Try
dill pickle perfume?

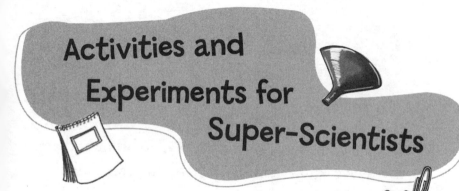

Activities and
Experiments for
Super-Scientists

Contents

Your Own Lab • 68

What? You Mean There's a *Method*? • 70

Snoop-O-Scope for Spies Like You:
Sound and Amplification • 72

Send a Secret Message: Codes and Cyphers • 75

Your Own Little World: Ecosystems • 77

Build Your Own Handy-Dandy
Paper Clip Picker-Upper
(otherwise known as an electromagnet) • 83

T Minus 30 Minutes and Counting:
Resonance • 89

Your Own Lab

You have an idea. A brilliant idea. So brilliant that life as we know it will never be the same again! You rush to your lab, anxious to prove your idea, boil solutions, and scribble in your lab notebook, except . . . *you don't have a lab.* Egads! Remember, good scientists are always prepared. So be prepared for all your brilliant ideas by creating your own lab. Here's how:

1. Clear a space in your bedroom, in a spare room, or in the attic—wherever your parents say it's okay. Add a card table, a chair, and—Great Scott!—you have a laboratory!

2. Begin collecting items that might be useful later. Magnets, clean jars with lids, string, straws, tape, paper clips, measuring cups, plastic utensils—you get the idea. And, of course, all good scientists must have a pair of safety glasses.

3. No top-notch scientist is complete without a lab coat. You can use a white button-down shirt (ask first!), and write your name on the front with a permanent marker.

4. Last but not least, you'll need a lab notebook. Any spiral or bound notebook is good. Jot your name in pen on your notebook, sharpen your pencil, and you're ready for your next brilliant idea! Observations, calculations, hypotheses, and results— record everything in your lab notebook.

A good lab notebook contains
1) Experiment title
2) Method (what you plan to do)
3) Hypothesis (what you think will happen)
4) Procedure (what you did, step by step)
5) Observations (what you saw)
6) Results (what actually happened)
7) Conclusion (based upon the results, was your hypothesis correct? Why or why not?)

What? You Mean There's a *Method*?

That's right, there's a method to the madness. It's called the **scientific method**, to be precise. In fact, scientists all over the world use the same method.

First, scientists observe. They examine. They peer. They scribble their observations in their lab notebooks (or type them into their computers, as the case may be).

Second, based on their observations, scientists develop a **hypothesis**, like Drake and Nell did in trying to determine the identity of the ghosts and ghouls haunting Edgar's house. Drake and Nell's hypothesis was simply their best guess as to what was causing the noise. It probably sounded something like this: "We believe the haunting of Edgar's home is being caused by the amplification of sound through the old pipes. We further believe that Poe is the culprit."

Third, scientists test their hypothesis. (After all, maybe the hypothesis is correct, but maybe it isn't. Maybe there really *are* ghosts and ghouls! Yikes!) In testing their hypothesis, scientists follow a **procedure**. In the following experiments and activities, you will also follow a procedure. It is important to read through the instructions and set out all of the needed materials before beginning the experiment. So whip out your lab notebooks, sharpen those pencils, put on those lab coats, and prepare to join the masses of scientists everywhere!

Good Science Tip

To avoid mixing things up, all brilliant scientists label what they are working on. Usually masking tape and a pen or marker work fine for labeling. But if an experiment or the equipment gets wet or collects moisture, the ink might smudge or run or disappear entirely. To prevent that from happening, many scientists use a fine-point permanent marker, which won't wipe off except with alcohol.

Snoop-O-Scope for Spies Like You: Sound and Amplification

Egads! Your #1 enemy is holding a top secret meeting with your #2 enemy! Unless you listen in and stop their dastardly plot, horrible things are bound to happen. There's no time to lose! Build a Snoop-O-Scope so you can listen around corners.

MATERIALS

- 4-foot section of ¾-inch-diameter PVC pipe
- large funnel, such as the kind used for draining the oil from a car (make sure it's clean)
- duct tape
- two ¾-inch-diameter PVC elbows

PROCEDURE

1. Have an adult cut the pipe into two lengths: 1 foot and 3 foot (doesn't have to be exact).

2. Insert the pointed end of the funnel into one end of the 1-foot section of pipe. Secure with tape.

3. Insert one of the elbows onto the other end of the 1-foot pipe.

4. Fit the 3-foot section of pipe into the remaining hole of the same elbow and secure with tape. The pipe sections should now form a right angle to each other.

5. Finally, fit the last elbow onto the open end of the 3-foot pipe. This is for your listening pleasure and comfort. (Spy work should be comfy whenever possible.)

6. To activate, simply stick the funnel end around a corner, and fit your ear snugly against the open hole of the elbow. Listen carefully and be prepared for action. (Beware: Do not alert archenemies to your presence.)

More Cool Stuff: Have a friend stand around the corner and whisper softly as you listen without using your Snoop-O-Scope. How well can you hear her? Then, have her whisper the same thing at the same volume, except now use your Snoop-O-Scope. Is there a difference? (If you are sad and lonely and have no friends, try this activity using a radio, stereo, or iPod.)

Did You Know?

Before electronic hearing aids were invented, people who were hard-of-hearing used *ear trumpets*. An ear trumpet was a trumpet-shaped device designed to amplify sound waves by funneling sound into the ear of the listener. Your Snoop-O-Scope works by the same principle.

Send a Secret Message Codes and Cyphers

You're taking a pleasant stroll along the wetland path. Suddenly—aliens invade! Send a secret message to warn your partner! Here's how:

MATERIALS

- 3 index cards
- scissors
- pencil
- eraser

PROCEDURE

1. Cut out five or six rectangles here and there from an index card. Make a second index card just like it. (These are your master code keys. They should look exactly alike. You keep one; your partner gets the other.)

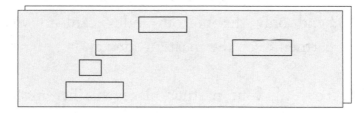

2. To write a message, place your master copy over a blank index card. Write your code through

the holes onto the blank index card, using one word per rectangle.

3. Uncover the bottom index card. You should have five or six words on the card. Now fill in the rest of the note by including those words in sentences. (Erase and start over if it doesn't sound natural.)

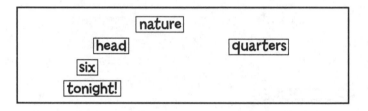

4. Send only the bottom index card to your partner. Keep the master code key.

5. To read, your partner places his/her master copy over the index card. The code words will show through the rectangles to reveal the secret message: **Nature Headquarters, six tonight!**

Your Own Little World: Ecosystems

Have you ever wanted to create your own little world? Be "master of the universe," so to speak? In this activity, you can create your own little world by building a terrarium. A terrarium is a miniature ecosystem (a place where plants and animals interact with one another and with their environment, including water, light, soil, and climate). It's fun and easy to do. Here's how:

MATERIALS

- fishbowl or similar clear container— big enough to allow you to easily put your hand through the opening
- pea-sized gravel, such as the kind used for the bottom of a fish tank
- large spoon (for scooping charcoal and soil)
- charcoal, such as the kind used in fish tank filters—find at pet stores
- potting soil (buy organic *sterilized* soil as it won't have fungi and molds)

- measuring cup
- mixing bowl
- two to three slow-growing, water-loving plants that won't grow too big (such as small ferns, nerve plant, false aralia, pink polka-dot plant, pilea, mini African violet, gloxinias, hepaticus, coleuses)
- paper towels
- cool stuff like rocks, ceramic frogs, gnomes, ninja warriors . . . (optional)
- plastic wrap
- rubber band
- scissors

PROCEDURE

1. Wash the fishbowl with warm soapy water. Rinse and dry completely.

2. Add gravel to the bottom of the fishbowl until it is ½ inch to ¾ inch deep.

3. With the spoon, scoop ¼ inch of charcoal over the gravel. Level it out in an even layer.

4. Pour approximately four cups of soil into the mixing bowl (*not* the fishbowl!) and stir in some water (about ⅔ cup). The soil should be damp enough so that it remains in a ball after you squeeze it. If it crumbles, add more water. If water drips out, add more soil.

5. Spoon in enough of the dampened soil to fill up to ⅓ or ½ of the fishbowl.

6. Decide where you want your plants. For each plant, dig a small hole (don't go too deep or you'll hit the charcoal), and then set the plant in the hole. Cover the roots with 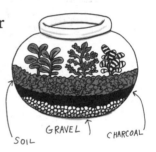 soil and pat the soil firmly so the plant stays in place. Repeat with your other plants. Don't be afraid to add more soil, if needed.

7. Carefully clean the inside of the glass with paper towels.

8. Add a few small handfuls of water. (Sprinkle it from your hand rather than pouring it in. This is gentler on the plants' delicate roots.)

9. Add your cool stuff if you want. Perhaps a ninja warrior hiding behind a fern? Or a ceramic frog sitting on a rock? Up to you.

10. Cover the opening with plastic wrap and secure with a rubber band. Trim the plastic wrap with scissors if it's too big.

11. Set your terrarium in a warm place where it will receive plenty of "indirect" light (not directly in the sun).

12. Sit back and watch the plants grow, oh you master of the universe, you.

Terrariums need just the right amount of moisture, so they are neither too wet nor too dry. So how do you determine the right amount of moisture? Here's a hot tip: if, after two days, moisture droplets (called **condensation**) form on the *sides of the glass* and obstruct your view, your terrarium is *too wet*. Remove the plastic wrap for a day or two and let it dry out.

If, after two days, there isn't any condensation forming on the *underside of the plastic top*, your terrarium is *too dry*. Add a *little* more water and cover it back up.

The moisture content of your terrarium is perfect when water droplets form on the underside of the plastic top, while the glass sides of the fishbowl remain clear. A terrarium with just the right amount of water will only need to be watered every 2–3 months. Also, trim any plants that grow too big.

How Does This Work?

Regular potted plants must be watered frequently because the water turns into a vapor, like cool steam, and escapes into the air. This process is known as evaporation. But because a terrarium's environment is enclosed, evaporating water cannot escape. So when vapor touches something, like the underside of the plastic, it forms condensation, or moisture droplets. Eventually the condensation drips on the plants like rain. This is called precipitation. A terrarium is just like a real ecosystem with a cycle of:

EVAPORATION

CONDENSATION

PRECIPITATION

Did You Know?

An alien species has invaded New Zealand and certain areas of the United States! It's called **purple loosestrife**, and it's a real noxious weed, much like "purple loosegoose." Although pretty, purple loosestrife is a non-native plant that clogs waterways and marshlands, starving wildlife by choking out other plants. Nicknamed "Marsh Monster," it has already caused millions of dollars' worth of damage in Oregon, Washington, and Idaho. But, all is not lost! Just like in the Doyle and Fossey episode, there are beetles called *Galerucella* that find purple loosestrife quite delicious. Scientists have released *Galerucella* into infested areas where the beetles chomp away. After a year of chomping, the ecosystem is back in balance! Beetles like *Galerucella* are called **biocontrol agents**.

Build Your Own Handy-Dandy Paper Clip Picker-Upper!

(otherwise known as an electromagnet)

You've had a long day. You're so wiped you don't have the energy to pick up a few paper clips.

But wait! Help is on the way! You can build your own Handy-Dandy Paper Clip Picker-Upper, otherwise known as an electromagnet! (But, you ask in confusion, doesn't building an electromagnet take energy? Well, why, ahem, yes it does, but it's fun, it's easy, so what the heck.)

MATERIALS

- 3 inch × 3 inch piece of cardboard or card stock (doesn't have to be exact)
- 2 brass paper fasteners
- 20 metal paper clips
- clear tape
- wire strippers (ask an adult for help when learning how to use these)

- 22-gauge insulated copper wire
- 4 alligator clips
- 9-volt battery
- one 4-inch to 5-inch steel or iron nail

PROCEDURE

1. Punch a hole in the cardboard about 1 inch from one of the edges.

2. Insert one of the paper fasteners through the hole (spread out the arms on the back).

3. Unfold a paper clip halfway. Slip the short arm of the paper clip around the head of the paper fastener.

4. Punch a second hole into the cardboard far enough away from the first hole so that when the second paper fastener is inserted, only the long arm of the paper clip can touch the second fastener. The short arm should be, well, ahem, too short.

5. On the back side of the cardboard, tape down the arms of both paper fasteners, making sure they don't touch each other. Turn the cardboard over, paper clip-side up, and tape the cardboard to a flat surface (table, kitchen counter, etc.) to secure it. This is your switch.

6. Using the wire stripper, cut a 12-inch piece of insulated wire. Strip about 1 inch of insulation off each end of the wire (ask an adult to show you how). Attach an alligator clip to each end by inserting the bare wire through the hole in the clip and wrapping it around the clip a few times.

7. Now connect one end of the wire to the positive battery terminal (if it's not labeled, either terminal is fine as long as you connect one wire per terminal, creating a complete circuit) and the other end to one of the paper fasteners.

8. Cut a second piece of insulated wire, about 2½ feet long. Again, strip the ends and attach the alligator clips. Wrap the wire tightly about 20 times around the nail, leaving at least 8 inches of loose wire at each end.

9. Connect one end of the wire to the negative battery terminal (again, if the battery isn't labeled, just use the opposite terminal), and the other end to the remaining paper fastener.

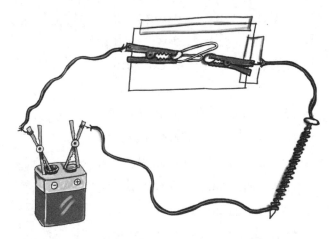

10. Ta-da! Congratulations! You have now completed your own Handy-Dandy Paper Clip Picker-Upper! Gigantic applause PLEASE!

11. Whoops ... You still need to turn on the switch in order to complete the electrical circuit. (Remember Frisco? He had his hand in his pocket? Switch on. Switch off. On. Off.) To turn the switch on, press down on the large arm of the paper clip so that it touches the second brass fastener. Your circuit is now complete, and your electromagnet is active. When you want to deactivate it, simply release the switch.

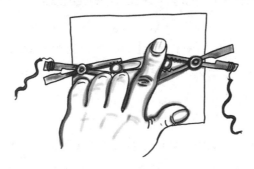

12. See how many paper clips you can pick up using your electromagnet.

Warning #1: Keep magnet away from DVDs, CDs, audiotapes, electronic devices, and computers, as it may damage them.

Warning #2: Magnets can release some of their energy in the form of heat. If your magnet becomes too warm, disconnect it until it cools off. Always disconnect it when not in use.

More Cool Stuff:

1. The strength of your magnet depends upon how many coils of wire you wrap around the nail. Using varying lengths of wire, coil it 10 times, 25 times, 50 times. . . . Write a hypothesis as to what you think will happen, and then test your hypothesis. Were you correct?

2. The size of the nail also affects magnet strength. Write a hypothesis, and then test it using different sized nails.

3. How can you bypass the switch to your electromagnet like Drake did under Shady Jim's booth? Test your hypothesis.

4. Instead of paper clips, try iron filings (ask at an auto-mechanic shop—they usually have iron filings for free, or you can buy a jar full from www.dowlingmagnets.com).

T Minus 30 Minutes and Counting: Resonance

It's T minus 30 minutes. The weather is simply ghastly, and the parade is about to begin. Soon it will march down Main Street, past Barko's Supermart and Iggy's Ice Cream Parlor . . . marching toward Mossy Lake Bridge . . . and *disaster!* It's up to you, Horace Peabody or Polly Plum (choose one), to save the day! But first you must develop a hypothesis:

"I believe the Mossy Lake Bridge is going bananas because _____." (Hint: If you can't think of a hypothesis, reread parade/bridge/bananas scene.)

Then you must build a simulation to test your hypothesis. Here's how:

MATERIALS

- 2 chairs
- string
- scissors

- 2 cedar hanger rings (circular cedar discs with hole cut in middle, available at department stores or online; if you can't find any, use a substitute such as old CDs)
- hair dryer

PROCEDURE

1. Place the chairs back to back.

2. Cut a piece of string approximately 10 feet long. Tie one end of the string to the back of one of the chairs.

3. Thread the string through the center of the two cedar hanger rings, and tie the other end of the string to the back of the other chair. Adjust the distance between the two chairs so that the string forms a "bridge," with the cedar rings hanging in the center of the bridge. There should be plenty of slack.

4. Standing beside the bridge, pull the cedar rings toward you and let go. The bridge should swing back and forth in a large arc, gradually becoming weaker before eventually stopping.

5. Try #4 again, except this time clap your hands every time the bridge is closest to you. Notice how the rhythm of your clapping stays the same, regardless of how big or small the arc of the swinging bridge is. *This rhythm is the natural frequency of the bridge.*

6. Again pull the cedar rings toward you and let go. Now, using the hair dryer, blast the cedar rings with air every time they move away from you (as if you were pushing someone on a swing, pushing the person away from you as the swing moves away). What happens? (Remember, this is called **resonance**. You are adding a force at the same frequency, which creates more vibration.)

7. Try the same thing again, except this time blast the cedar rings with air every time they move *toward* you. What happens?

8. Pedal like mad to the parade and save the day. Congratulations! You are a hero!

Check This Out!

From the moment it was built in 1940, the Tacoma Narrows Bridge had a severe case of the hiccups. On a windy day only four months after it was completed, "Galloping Gertie" collapsed into Puget Sound. Watch the video at: http://www.youtube.com/watch?v=3mclp9QmCGs. How would you like to try to drive across *that??!! Yikes!!* (Note: If you have difficulty finding the video, simply go to www.youtube.com and search for "Tacoma Narrows Bridge.")